Men's Devotional

Bloodline Breaker

In 30 Days Become the Man Hell Hoped You would Never Be.

WILLIE G. MILLER JR.

TABLE OF CONTENTS

Appreciation

To my wife, Beverley

You are the quiet strength behind the war cry, the peace in my storm, and the answer to prayers I did not know how to pray. While *Bloodline Breaker* carries my voice, it was your love, support, and intercession that kept me steady through every page.

Thank you for believing in the assignment on my life even when it cost you comfort. For holding my arms up when I was fighting hell, and for reminding me who I was when warfare tried to make me forget.

This book breaks curses but you helped support the man bold enough to write it.

I honor and love you.

And I would not be this dangerous without you.

Let's keep shaking kingdoms together.

Bill

Dedication

To every man who was born into brokenness but refused to die in it.

To the sons who never met their fathers, and the fathers who never became sons.

To the young warriors still trying to make sense of the war inside.

To the ones who have been silent for too long, fighting battles nobody saw, bleeding in places nobody touched, and surviving storms that should have drowned you.

This is for you!

- You are the interruption.
- You are the answer.
- You are the man hell never saw coming.

And to the next generation of bloodline breakers, may this devotional be your fire, your strategy, and your weapon.

Let this be the book hell wishes you never opened.

Let this be the spark that lights up your legacy.

Willie G. Miller Jr.

Introduction

Let us keep it real. This is not your average devotional. This is not your "read a verse, sip your coffee, and feel better about being "broken" type of thing. This is a war manual. A blueprint for every man who refuses to let hell write the final chapter of his story.

I did not write this to inspire you. I wrote this to awaken you. Because deep down, you already know you are not built to be average. There is something in you that's always known you were different. Chosen! Marked! Dangerous! But life tried to bury it. Religion tried to mute it and trauma tried to kill it.

Guess what! It did not work! That is why you are holding this book. Because you are the interruption. You are the curse-breaker, the bloodline disrupter, the one hell has been dreading. You are not just trying to be a better man, you are about to become the man hell hoped you would never be.

These next 30 days, We are going in. I am not here to coddle you, I am here to confront the lies you have believed, the demons you have tolerated, and the cycles you have normalized. We are digging deep, praying hard, declaring truth, and walking in power.

No more excuses. No more playing soft. No more babysitting dysfunction. This is your activation season. So, let us be clear… You are not here by accident. You survived on purpose. You were built to break what broke your bloodline.

Let's go!

Bloodline

First things first. Understand, a bloodline is more than a biological lineage. It is a generational stream of identity, influence, and inheritance. Naturally, it traces ancestry and genetics; spiritually, it carries both blessings and burdens, including patterns of sin, trauma, or iniquity passed through family lines.

In biblical terms, bloodlines are conduits of covenant. Covenants that are legal in the spirit realm. They can grant authority, open doors, or create bondage, depending on whether they are godly or demonic. People can unknowingly enter ungodly covenants through trauma, sexual sin, idolatry, or even words.

While bloodlines pass down favor and legacy, others transmit cycles that must be broken through spiritual authority, repentance, and the power of deliverance. You were not just born into your family's last name; you were born into a battle. That is why breaking old covenants and stepping into Kingdom covenant is essential for freedom.

Today we step into a relationship with the one true and living God. We confess Jesus Christ as our God and savior and believe that God has raised Him from the dead! We initiate this relationship with Him and bind ourselves to Him and agree to walk in obedience, trust, and blessing as a true son of God.

Breaking Ungodly Covenants & Enter God's Covenant Alignment.

Declaration and prayer:

Father, in the name of Jesus, my Savior and Covenant Keeper I rise today in full authority as a blood-bought child of God.

I break agreement with every ungodly covenant, spoken or unspoken, known, or unknown, generational, or personal.

I renounce every demonic pact, every soul tie, every vow, every curse, and every cycle that did not come from You.

I cut the spiritual umbilical cord tying me to bloodline curses, witchcraft, trauma, sexual sin, idolatry, religion, rebellion, or anything that has had legal access to my life.

I cancel Satan's contracts with my name on them. Every word curse, every ritual, every altar raised against my destiny. I command it to fall by fire and never rise again. Let the blood of Jesus speak louder than every demonic accusation. Let the cross override every generational curse.

I now enter divine alignment with Jesus Christ. I accept and activate the covenant of grace, truth, sonship, kingship, priesthood and freedom through Jesus Christ.

I declare and decree: I belong to God. My bloodline is redeemed. My purpose is protected in Christ. My identity is sealed. I am no longer bound by history. I am commissioned by heaven to do the works of God.
In Jesus' mighty name, Amen.

Day 1: It Ends With Me.

Scripture Focus:
"Behold, I give unto you power to tread on serpents and scorpions, and over all the power of the enemy: and nothing shall by any means hurt you." —Luke 10:19

Hook:
You either break the cycle... or become it.

Devotional Thought:
Hell knew your bloodline was jacked up with cycles, secrets, and shame. So, it bet everything on you staying stuck. Thought you would repeat what ruined the ones before you. Thought you would cave like your uncle, disappear like your dad, and stay silent like your mom. But Hell forgot one thing, you are not them. You were not born to blend in with brokenness. You were raised up to end it.

One man watched his father drown in addiction and followed him into the same bottle until it buried them both. They became forgotten and dismissed. Then, there was another man who stared down the same demons...and chose war. Chose healing and freedom. They were from the same bloodline, but they chose a different outcome.

This is where curses come to die. Addiction? Crushed under Kingdom weight. Father wounds? Healed by the hands of the Father. Secret sin? Exposed and evicted with no right to return. You have Hell's eviction notice in your mouth and Kingdom fire in your bones.

So, stop nursing demons your ancestors tolerated. You were not born to be a hostage. You were forged to be a hammer. You are not a victim. You are the vengeance of Heaven. Say it and mean it: "It ends with me." Hell thought you'd fold but, God built you to finish it.

Reflection:
What curse dies because you woke up today?

Declaration:
I ain't babysitting bondage. I break it. I'm not my bloodline—I'm God's battle axe.

"Therefore, if any man be in Christ, he is a new creature..."
—*2 Corinthians 5:17*

Day 2: The Mirror Lied.

Scripture Focus:
"For we are His workmanship, created in Christ Jesus unto good works..." —Ephesians 2:10

Hook:
The mirror does not show the man. The war does.

Devotional Thought:
The mirror lied!

What you have been seeing is not truth, it is trauma in disguise. That reflection has been distorted by years of rejection, family failure, and abandonment. That is not your identity, that's just residue and the residue is not reality.

One boy stared in the mirror and saw everything his father did not say.... You are not enough, you are not worthy, and you were never chosen. So, that boy shrank to fit in with what his father never said about him. He became what he interpreted out of silence. He framed his identity in what he thought someone might be thinking about him. Unspoken words! There was another boy who experienced the same abandonment. The same heartbreak but, he decided to look again and saw a warrior in the wreckage. Same past, same pain. Different prophecy. You choose the unspoken words you hear your father saying because those words are prophecy you are speaking into your life.

You have been looking at yourself through cracked lenses for too long. They called you broken, cursed, and forgotten. But Heaven never echoed that nonsense. You are not what life labeled you.

You're what God crafted in His likeness and image.

- You carry the glory of God!
- You have the power to create and to tear down.
- You have dominion!

Heaven did not design you to be cute, compliant, or quiet. You are not some random project, you are a divine threat. Built by God with intention. Marked for destruction...of every stronghold that thought it had a right to your name.

So do not let your reflection punk you into shrinking. Look again and see the weapon God designed. See the assignment etched in your spirit. Then act like it!

Dominate!

Reflection:
What lies spoken or unspoken have you allowed to shape your identity?

Declaration:
I am not what I went through. I'm what God raised up. I'm a mirror-breaking, hell-shaking masterpiece.

"I will praise thee; for I am fearfully and wonderfully made..."
—*Psalm 139:14*

Day 3: Chains Do Not Fit Me Anymore.

Scripture Focus:
"Stand fast therefore in the liberty wherewith Christ hath made us free and be not entangled again with the yoke of bondage."
—Galatians 5:1

Hook:
You are not chained. You are just comfortable in captivity.

Devotional Thought:
Let us get one thing straight! Jesus did not bleed out on a cross for you to keep flirting with your chains. He did not get torn open by Roman whips so you could call bondage "just the way I am." That is not identity, that's captivity with makeup on.

One man kept going back to the same addiction that almost killed his father. The addiction was dressed and made up to look like a place of comfort. Masking pain, distance and spiritual dryness as peace, clarity, and identity. When questioned why, the man responded, "It's in my blood." Across the street there lived another man who was experiencing the same cravings with a different testimony. We asked why he chooses to stay away from his addictions he responded, "It might be in my blood—but I've got new DNA now." I am in Christ; I am a new creature. Those things have passed away and I choose to walk in the newness. Same temptation. Different testimony.

You are not stuck. You are sedated, numbed by culture, comfort, and compromise. That addiction has expired. The shame and dead weight attached to that soul tie is broken!

You've outgrown the struggle, but it is still squatting in your mind rent-free. Time to serve it notice and evict it! In Jesus name.

Understand, freedom is not a mood. It is not a vibe. It is a verdict. God has set you free indeed. No one, not even Satan can petition the courts of Heaven to change that. You were sentenced to walk in dominion, not depression. You are a King-Priest who has been crowned with purpose and not crushed by patterns. You are not some rehab project barely making it. You are the aftermath of Christ's resurrection power. So, stop dragging what Jesus already destroyed. Jesus paid it all when he died on the cross and rose again and hells got the receipts. We are the finish works of Christ.

Now walk like it is finished!

Reflection:
What are you still wearing that Jesus already buried?

Declaration:
I do not do chains, I do freedom! If Jesus broke it, I ain't picking it back up.

"If the Son therefore shall make you free, ye shall be free indeed."
—John 8:36

Day 4: Daddy Issues. Kingdom Answers.

Scripture Focus:
"A father to the fatherless, a defender of widows, is God in his holy dwelling." —Psalm 68:5 (NIV)

Hook:
Your absent father didn't disqualify you; it activated you.

Devotional Thought:
He left!
He failed!
He disappointed you!
So, what!

The throne is still occupied. God, the good father still sits on His throne!

Your earthly father may have walked out but God did not! The pain he caused was not designed to cripple and stop you in your tracks. It was a training ground to introduce you to the Father who never leaves or forsakes you.

One boy grew up angry, built walls, and swore he'd never become like his father, until he did! Different voice, different body, different generation but the same violence. Another boy experienced the same abandonment. When he looked into the mirror, he saw the same pain. He decided to break the mirror, shattered the grudge and the pain, and let God the father into places his dad never touched. Same story but a different answer.

Let's be clear, God is not Plan B. He is not the backup when "dad didn't work out." He is the original source. The blueprint. The beginning and the Builder.

Everything that I thought I missed out on with my dad; God gave me an upgrade. Understand, you were not built to be bitter. You were built to carry bloodline authority. So do not become the man who wounded you. When you mix bitterness with authority you become a controlling person instead of a person who covers others. You become a person who corrects without compassion, and you will use power to protect yourself instead of to serve others. Instead of those things, become the man he never had the courage to be.

You are not fatherless because God is your Father. You are Father-filled and that changes everything.

Reflection:
How has the absence of your father shaped the man you're becoming?

Declaration:
I forgive, I rise, and I lead. I am not fatherless! I am fueled and fathered by God the Father.

"When my father and my mother forsake me, then the Lord will take me up." —Psalm 27:10

Day 5: God is not Looking for Perfect Men.

Scripture Focus:
"But God hath chosen the foolish things of the world to confound the wise..." —1 Corinthians 1:27

Hook:
God's not intimidated by your mess. He specializes in it.

Devotional Thought:
God ain't checking your résumé. He's checking for surrender.

You keep thinking He is looking for swag, status, or spiritual giants who know everything. Nah, partner. Heaven isn't hiring performers. It's commissioning the broken, the bruised, and the barely-holding-on.

One man built his life trying to impress God with spiritual hustle. You know, that one with perfect prayers, clean Instagram verses, spotless church attendance. But he burned out fast and still felt empty. Then there was another man who was Raw, Wrecked, and Repentant with no filters. Just showed up and said, "God, I ain't much, but I'm yours." Same need. Different oil.

You might think you are too jacked up. Too inconsistent and flawed to carry something holy. Good! That means you are finally qualified. God built armies out of murderers, cowards, liars, and drunks. He took Moses the murderer with a stutter, David the King who killed a man and took his wife, Peter who cut the man's ear off and turned them into wrecking balls for the Kingdom.

So, stop faking holy. Stop trying to impress Heaven with highlight reels. You are not too far gone. You are just one real moment from your purpose. God does not anoint the perfect. He anoints those who are available. So, show up and say yes.

Reflection:
Where are you trying to earn what God already gave through grace?

Declaration:
I'm not performing. I'm positioning. I'm chosen, not perfect—and that's enough.

"My grace is sufficient for thee: for my strength is made perfect in weakness..." —2 Corinthians 12:9

Day 6: Stop Bowing to Porn.

Scripture Focus:
"I made a covenant with mine eyes; why then should I think upon a maid?" —Job 31:1

Hook:
Porn ain't pleasure. Its poison dressed in pixels.

Devotional Thought:
Porn isn't just a habit—it's a stronghold. It is an imagination that's exalting itself above and against the knowledge of God. Eventually it opens you up to demonic influence that has an agenda to abort the purpose of God in your life.

It does not just steal time. It hijacks your vision, sedates your spirit, and murders your authority in secret. Every click is breaking covenant with God. Every scroll is a seed and shame is its harvest. The trick is you began to think you are just watching images. Naaaah partner, you are inviting intruders into your soul. Open doors do not just entertain demons; they empower them and give them legal access. Stop clicking and close the doors.

One man scrolled himself numb and lost his marriage, dulled his calling, and couldn't pray without guilt choking him. Another man had the same addiction and urges. But he drew a line in the Spirit, got real, got ruthless, and reclaimed his mantle. His authority, status and identity in God. Same temptation. Different outcome.

God did not call you to be a slave to screens. He called you to be a man of fire and focus. A man who guards gates and governs atmospheres. The lust that has been running your life has an expiration date, and that date is now! It's time to make war, shut it down and take back your mind and desire system. You must protect your mantle. The Lord is waiting for your eyes to look at Him because your help to overcome comes from Him. Hell is banking on your silence. You choose who gets the last word.

Reflection:
Are you feeding a habit that's stealing your future?

Declaration:
I break every soul-tie and cancel every image that tried to own me. I am pure, focused, and free.

"Blessed are the pure in heart: for they shall see God."
—Matthew 5:8

Day 7: The Devil Knows Your Name.

Scripture Focus:
"And the evil spirit answered and said, Jesus I know, and Paul I know; but who are ye?" —Acts 19:15

Hook:
You weren't saved to be safe. You were born to be feared.

Devotional Thought:
Demons do not lose sleep over church boys who sing loud but live powerlessly. They are not shaking over dudes with Bibles in their hands but compromise in their hearts. But you! Oh, they know your name.

Hell takes a roll call every morning and your name echoes like a war drum. Because a Bloodline Breaker is not just quoting scripture to feel holy. He is walking like the Word is a weapon. He is swinging the truth like a sword. He is tearing down altars with his "yes."

One man memorized verses, sat in church, clapped on cue and still walked around spiritually invisible. While the other man with the same scriptures believed and lived them and became them. Now hell flinches every time his feet hit the floor. Same Bible, different authority.

Your life is a threat, and your obedience is a problem. Every time you submit, hell loses territory. Every time you stay pure, demons lose their grip. Every time you tell the truth, systems start shaking.

You were not put here to be polite. You were built to disrupt darkness so if hell is not scared of you yet, it will be!

Reflection:
Is your life making hell nervous... or comfortable?

Declaration:
I'm known in heaven and feared in hell. I move with power, not permission.

"Resist the devil, and he will flee from you." —*James 4:7*

Day 8: Break the Blood Oath.

Scripture Focus:
"Christ hath redeemed us from the curse of the law, being made a curse for us..." —Galatians 3:13

Hook:
You were born with a curse—but you've been reborn with a contract.

Devotional Thought:
You inherited some stuff you never signed up for:
- Rage.
- Pride.
- Fear.
- Promiscuity.
- Poverty.

That was not just "how your family is." That was a demonic contract written in pain, sealed in silence, and passed down like inheritance. But then Jesus stepped in and when His blood hit your name, hell's legal rights got revoked. You are not just forgiven; you have been transferred from curse to covenant. From dysfunction to dominion.

One man wore his family trauma like armor and called it personality, passed it to his kids, and called it "survival." Another man from the same bloodline with the same mess tore up the old paperwork, went to the courts of Heaven, and rewrote the story. Same history but one of the two chose a different covenant. Understand, your DNA has been re-coded by the cross and your identity isn't genetic, it's prophetic.

The devil may know your past, but he cannot touch your purpose. He saw how you were raised, he just did not see you would rise. So, rip up the old agreements, renounce the trash you tolerated. Break the oath. Burn the script and sign the new covenant…in the blood of Jesus. Never forget, you do not owe hell anything.

Reflection:
What bloodline contract do you need to renounce *today*?

Declaration:
Every curse is broken. Every demon is denied. I live under a covenant, not a contract.

"No weapon that is formed against thee shall prosper…" —*Isaiah 54:17*

Day 9: Emotional Authority.

Scripture Focus:
"He that is slow to anger is better than the mighty; and he that ruleth his spirit than he that taketh a city." —Proverbs 16:32

Hook:
If your emotions run you—hell already owns you.

Devotional Thought:
Let's go ahead and say it plain: You cannot cast out what you keep cuddling. Some of y'all are not demon-possessed, you are just emotionally undisciplined. Every trigger you justify, every mood swing, you excuse, and every offense you rehearse is not personality. That is an open door.

One man blamed his temper on his zodiac sign and blew up his relationships, lost jobs, and called it "just how I process." Another man with the same fire inside decided to hand it over to the Holy Ghost, forged discipline in the furnace, and now he does not just feel, he rules! Both men dealt with the same emotions, but each had a different outcome.

A man who won't master his emotions is a grenade with no pin and is dangerous to everyone around him, especially himself. But you brother; weren't called to be ruled by feelings. You were built to lead with spiritual authority. Peace ain't a vibe, it's your posture.

Self-control is your superpower so, do not let your emotions punk you out of your elevation. Do not let mood swings hijack your mantle. Understand, real power starts with self-governance and a Kingdom man knows how to rule himself before he tries to rule anything else.

Reflection:
What emotion has been driving you more than the Holy Spirit?

Declaration:
My emotions don't control me, I command them. I lead with truth, not temper.

"For God hath not given us the spirit of fear; but of power, and of love, and of a sound mind." —2 Timothy 1:7

Day 10: You're Not Soft, You're Set Apart.

Scripture Focus:
"Come out from among them, and be ye separate, saith the Lord..."
—2 Corinthians 6:17

Hook:
You're not weird, you're wired different.

Devotional Thought:
Let them talk. "You're too deep." "Too holy." "Too extra."

Good!

You were not built to blend in with basic. You were not wired to be liked by lukewarm people living half-saved and half-lost.

One man shrunk to fit in and dumbed down his walk, laughed at what grieved his spirit, and kept it "chill" to stay accepted. Another man who was under the same pressure. But he chose consecration over clout. He stood alone until his stand shook others free. Similar calling but different courage.

You are not soft because you do not chase bodies, burn blunts, or act recklessly. You are not fragile because you lead with purity, purpose, and restraint. You are dangerous because you are set apart. The world wants clones. God's raising up demon slayers. Those men with oil in their veins, fire in their mouths, and conviction in their chest. Men who will not flinch in the face of darkness.

Men who carry thunder but walk in peace. So do not dilute who you are just to make cowards comfortable. They did not save you. They do not sustain or define you.

You are God's problem for darkness. So, walk and move like the weapon you are!

Reflection:
Where have you been shrinking to fit what God called you to confront?

Declaration:
I am set apart. I am on assignment. I refuse to apologize for being anointed.

"But ye are a chosen generation, a royal priesthood... that ye should show forth the praises of Him..." —1 Peter 2:9

Day 11: Get Your Mind Back.

Scripture Focus:
"And be not conformed to this world: but be ye transformed by the renewing of your mind..." —Romans 12:2

Hook:
Your hands won't change until your head does.

Devotional Thought:
You cannot break, what still owns your thoughts. The devil is not just after your behavior; He is hunting for your agreement. If he can hijack your head, he can paralyze your purpose.

One man kept saying, "I'm just tired and stressed." Meanwhile, his mind was a war zone, anxiety on loop, doubt and fear running wild, and his identity shattered. Meanwhile another man in the next cell was experiencing the same pressure. But he decided to evict the lies and rebuilt his thoughts with truth. He took back his mental territory. He understood that if he allowed those thoughts to stay, he would become them. We are a product of what we think. The bible says, as a man thinks so is he. The same attack was launched but with a different outcome.

The enemy's strategy is surgical:
- Distract you!
- Defeat you!

Fill your head with so much junk that you implode before you ever step into your assignment.

Let us be clear, God did not give you a mind just to survive. He gave you a mind to build. To give birth to the blueprints to build and frame by faith. To lead in clarity while the world drowns in confusion. It is time to stop babysitting mental clutter. Change the narrative and stop calling stress "just part of life." Because it is not. It is bondage in disguise!

Remember, you have Kingdom access. The mind of Christ is your default thought, the foundation that you build all your thoughts on! It is not your backup plan; it is your first and only option! If you want your life to level up— your thinking must go up first. This is not a suggestion. This is a hostile takeover. You must break yourself into a position of letting the mind of God be in you! The time is now! Get your mind back and do not apologize for the violence it takes to break you.

Reflection:
What thought pattern do you need to evict today?

Declaration:
My mind is not a playground for hell. I think like Heaven. I build like God.

"Let this mind be in you, which was also in Christ Jesus..."
—*Philippians 2:5*

Day 12: Kill the Excuses.

Scripture Focus:
"A little sleep, a little slumber, a little folding of the hands to sleep: So shall thy poverty come as one that travelleth..."
—Proverbs 6:10–11

Hook:
You can make excuses, or you can make war! But not both.

Devotional Thought:
Excuses are demons in disguise. Clever lies dressed up to sound logical. "I'm tired." "I'll do it tomorrow." "I'm not ready yet." Nah, unacceptable! You are not under review waiting for a stamp of approval. You are already called, chosen, and dangerous!

One man kept explaining his delay. He had potential, ideas, vision... but no execution. Life moved on and purpose passed him by. His coworker experienced the same exhaustion and some of the same battles. But he refused to babysit his comfort. He showed up bloody, tired, stretched, and God met him there. They had the same capacity to dream but had distinct levels of commitment.

Heaven is not recruiting excuse-makers. God is raising up assassins. Men who do not negotiate with procrastination. Men who show up when it is hard, hidden, or hellish. You must realize, every excuse you nurture is a sword you drop. Every delay you justify is "Kingdom territory" surrendered.

God's not waiting for your perfect plan. He is waiting for your *yes and your grind*. It takes zero talent to work hard. So, if you really want freedom, get it. If you really want to lead, get up and move.

Excuses do not just stall your progress... They assassinate your calling and purpose.

How about this, Kill them first!

Reflection:
What excuse do you need to assassinate today?

Declaration:
No more delays. No more comfort zones. I kill what keeps me average.

"I can do all things through Christ which strengtheneth me." — *Philippians 4:13*

Day 13: You are Not a Simp, You are a Soldier.

Scripture Focus:
"Thou therefore endure hardness, as a good soldier of Jesus Christ."
—2 Timothy 2:3

Hook:
Weak men fold. Kingdom men fight.

Devotional Thought:
A simp hands his strength to people who mock his spirit. He trades power for attention, and purpose for a pat on the back. He puts excessive attention, time, energy, or emotional investment into someone who does not reciprocate it, usually out of a desperate desire for approval, validation, or affection. But a soldier, guards his heart like a vault, and moves like a man on assignment.

One brother posted thirst traps, said all the right lines, chasing approval like it was oxygen, and still felt empty when the lights went off. The other brother with the same hunger to be seen decided to be quiet and dig deep. He chose warfare over validation, and now he is not chasing influence, he is carrying fire. The consuming fire of God. These guys had the same desire but different decisions and different discipline.

Come on Boss! You were not born to beg for likes. You were built for battle. You do not need culture to clap for you! To hell with standing ovations, you need Heaven to move. The devil does not flinch at your smooth talk. He fears your secret place and your intercession. He fears your fire-tested "yes." It's time to stop simping for culture and start training like a conqueror.

Holiness is not soft, it is savage. You must crucify yourself. It gets nasty! Discipline is not weakness; it is weaponized willpower. Love is not passive; it is protective power. You are not less of a man because you are righteous. You are more of a threat because of it.

Reflection:
Where have you lowered your standard just to feel seen?

Declaration:
I am not out here begging for validation. I am a soldier who is trained, tested, and trusted.

"Watch ye, stand fast in the faith, quit you like men, be strong."
—*1 Corinthians 16:13*

Day 14: Worship is War.

Scripture Focus:
"Let the high praises of God be in their mouth, and a two-edged sword in their hand;" —Psalm 149:6

Hook:
Real worship does not just lift hands—it wrecks strongholds.

Devotional Thought:
You thought worship was soft. Nah Bruh. Worship is war. You might have tears in your eyes, but it is not an emotional filler, it is spiritual fire. Worship is transactional and transformational. It is the time where you experience a transformational change in your identity. During this transaction, God exchanges your identity and replaces it with His identity.

Understand this! Every time you praise, you swing a sword. Every shout is not just noise; it is a knockout punch. When you praise, you invite God to inhabit your praise and occupy space or residence in what you release out of your mouth in response to His greatness, His power, His authority, and majesty. Every lifted hand puts hell on notice that you are sounding a war cry to invite the God of war into your space and situation.

One man stood silent in service, arms crossed, too cool to lift his hands, he would stand and watch as others engaged in worship. He stood in silence reflecting on his problems and how he really needed God to help with his situations while demons danced over his silence. Crazy right! Yeah Bruh, devils come to church too! Then there was this other brother. He was fighting some of the same battles, but he worshiped like the war was real because it was. He openly looked to the hills to where he knew his help would come from. He understood his help comes from God and every time he opened his mouth, hell got nervous. Those brothers stood in the same atmosphere Sunday after Sunday but the one who worshiped had a different authority and a different encounter with God.

Worship is how real men bleed without breaking. How warriors breathe when they are under pressure. How Kingdom assassins reload in the middle of a fight. You don't need pretty vocals and eloquent words; you need violent surrender. You need unapologetic reverence for God. Understanding that everything pales in comparison to God. Nothing that I have or could ever achieve compares to His presence in my life! He is God! He has all power, and all glory belongs to Him. He was not created! He simply IS!

When you worship, you realign Heaven and earth; and disrupt hell. When you do not feel like worshiping, that is the exact moment to go wild. Because silence is consent and hell banks on yours. So, lift your voice like chains are breaking. Raise your hands like altars are falling. Start moving your body like a breakthrough is not optional because it's not. This is warfare! This is worship! This is how we win and how we reign with Christ.

Reflection:
Are you worshiping with a whisper when the moment demands a war cry?

Declaration:
My worship is warfare. My praise is a problem for hell.

"Out of the mouth of babes and sucklings hast thou ordained strength..." —Psalm 8:2

Day 15: Own Your Lane.

Scripture Focus:
"Let every man abide in the same calling wherein he was called."
—1 Corinthians 7:20

Hook:
You'll never win running someone else's race.

Devotional Thought:
Comparison is the cancer of calling. It does not just distract, it destroys. Every scroll, every highlight reel, and every curated post on social media whispers the same lie: "You're behind." But let us get something straight: You weren't built to compete; you were built to dominate your lane.

One man spent his life chasing others, mimicking their moves, echoing their words, dying by their applause. He watched every social media post. He was distracted and followed what others were doing. Before he realized it, he started hoping they would not outshine him. The other guy turned his attention inward and focused on his assignment, tuned out the noise, and moved with Heaven's backing. He realized, comparison is the doorway to insecurity. He decided not to provide a pathway for insecurity into his life. He shut it down. Both had the same potential but one took a different posture and maintained his place in God.

Your oil flows where your obedience lives. Not in imitation and envy of others. But in alignment. So, stop chasing what is not yours and measuring yourself against men who are not built like you. God gave you your own fingerprint because your assignment is unmatched. God does not run out of original ideas, concepts, and methodologies.

What he has for you is for you. Brother! man, it is time to be obsessed with your purpose, not someone else's applause. Hell hopes you will stay distracted. Do not fall for it!

Reflection:
Where have you allowed comparison to rob your confidence?

Declaration:
I am not in competition. I am in covenant. I run my race, and I win.

"Looking unto Jesus the author and finisher of our faith..." — *Hebrews 12:2*

Day 16: Stop Sleeping on Yourself.

Scripture Focus:
"Awake thou that sleepest, and arise from the dead, and Christ shall give thee light." —Ephesians 5:14

Hook:
You've been praying for a breakthrough, but God's been waiting for a *wake-up*.

Devotional Thought:
Some of y'all are not stuck, you are just spiritually asleep. You've heard the Word. You know the truth. But you're still hitting snooze on your destiny. The enemy does not need to kill you if he can just keep you numb. If he can soothe you in comfort, he's already won half the battle. Get Up! Let's Go! Game ON!

One man knew his calling. He had been dreaming about it for days, months, and years but kept delaying. God would wake him early in the morning with things that He needed him to do. He would not take any action because in his mind, he was waiting for the "right time." Years passed, and so did his purpose. Now he stands on the sideline of life watching his friend's success in God. Yeah, that dude he used to talk to about all his dreams decided to wake up! He experienced some of the same obstacles but mustered up the faith to trust God and stepped into his assignment with fire. They had the same potential and opportunity but one took a different posture and now he is realizing God's dream and purpose for his life.

You're not just a man; you're a move of God. You don't need another confirmation, you need confrontation. It's time to confront your complacency. Come on man! It is time to get in the game. You are a vital piece on God's chess board. Shake yourself and get in position. God's not going to drag you, He's calling you and if you don't move now, you'll forfeit the future that's begging for your "yes."

It's time to rise!
It's time to roar!

Let hell know you're up!

Reflection:
What part of you is still asleep when God is calling you to move?

Declaration:
I'm wide awake. I'm alert. I move with urgency and power.

"Redeeming the time, because the days are evil." —Ephesians 5:16

Day 17: You're Not the Victim, You're the Vengeance.

Scripture Focus:
"Vengeance is mine; I will repay, saith the Lord."
—Romans 12:19

Hook:
You weren't saved to cry over the wound—you were saved to wage war.

Devotional Thought:
Victimhood is a cage for someone who has been hurt, wronged, or attacked physically, emotionally, mentally, or spiritually. Vengeance is a call. Not to repay evil for evil but to rise and flip the script. Hell thought trauma would take you out. God's using it to send you in.

This man went through a bad divorce. His wife cheated on him, turned his children against him and caused him public shame. He wore his wounds like a badge of honor rehearsing the pain, reliving the betrayal, it became his identity. He did not know he was living with a victim mindset and was trapped. He was locked into blame, shame, and delay. One day he bumped into another guy who experienced the same situation and had some of the same scares. He questioned him, asking how he moved on from the betrayal. He responded, "I let the pain push me into my purpose." He said, "I stopped nursing my wounds and started wielding the weapon." Same history but different destiny.

You are not what happened to you. You are what rises after it. Let the scars remind you that you survived. Now you conquer. Stop rehearsing your wounds. You have be tried in the fire now, start activating your assignment. Face it, you're not just healed. You are the weapon, and you are dangerous!

Reflection:
Where have you been replaying pain instead of repurposing it?

Declaration:
I'm not the victim. I'm the vengeance. I will use every wound as a weapon.

"They overcame him by the blood of the Lamb, and by the word of their testimony…" —*Revelation 12:11*

Day 18: Don't Date a Distraction.

Scripture Focus:
"Be ye not unequally yoked together with unbelievers..."
—2 Corinthians 6:14

Hook:
Your purpose is too heavy to hitch it to a lightweight.

Devotional Thought:
Every woman in your inbox isn't your assignment. Some are traps with lashes, pretty feet, and manicured hands, while others are mirrors reflecting your dysfunction. Let's keep it real, God didn't call you to flirt with distractions or hook up with a liability; he called you to build with a helpmate.

One man kept chasing curves, skirts and compliments. He got some attention, got some women but lost authority. Every time a woman in boxed him, he responded by opening and connecting himself to them.   Putting down the vision and purpose for his life.   Man! Bruh, talking about bad booty!   That would be any booty that separates me from God and my purpose. Then there was another man who struggled with the same cravings and same inbox. He decided to shut the door and clear out the noise, and wait for a woman who could birth legacy, not just moments. He understood that he could not risk planting his seed into soil that may not be able to provide an environment for his legacy to flourish and be sustained for a lifetime and into the next. Same options with different choices led to a different outcome.

Your future is too massive to waste in fake intimacy. You don't need another DM dopamine hit, you need divine alignment. Don't date someone who feeds your lust but starves your spirit. She might be sexy, bondage isn't. Don't marry pretty dysfunction just because she's fine but unsubmitted. Who you link up with will either fuel your fire or drain your destiny. Choose with warfare in mind, not weakness in heart. Because every connection is either a covenant or a coffin.

Reflection:
Is your love life helping or hijacking your legacy?

Declaration:
I won't settle. I won't stumble. I choose covenant over compromise.

"He that findeth a wife findeth a good thing, and obtaineth favour of the Lord." —Proverbs 18:22

Day 19: You've Got Oil on You.

Scripture Focus:
"But the anointing which ye have received of him abideth in you..."
—1 John 2:27

Hook:
You're not regular. You're ruined for normal.

Devotional Thought:
You are not common, you are consecrated. Set apart, dedicated, and marked for divine use! You do not fit in because you were not built to. There's oil on your life! You are undeniable, unexplainable, undeniably dangerous! Heaven has stamped you with power and purpose. Your calling is loud. Hope you are listening! Your presence is prophetic, and your silence is costly.

I remember this man I meant a while back; he would always minimize who he was. He put himself into small spaces because he did not see himself the way God sees him. He spent his life shrinking his talent, downplaying the anointing on his life trying to fit into rooms God never told him to enter. He called it "humility," but it was really fear. As he looked around at his peers with similar anointing and callings, he watched as they walked in holy confidence. Instead of downplaying their anointing, they weaponized it. They had the same favor from God but experienced different fire.

That oil on your life will make you misunderstood. It will make you a target. But it will also make you unstoppable. Hell cannot duplicate it, and religion cannot explain it. But for Heavens sake, you need to trust it! So, stop dumbing down your assignment just to stay comfortable. Stop calling your intensity "too much." You're not too much, you are just enough to destroy every devil tied to your destiny. Walk like you are stamped and move like you are marked with power and authority.

Reflection:
Where have you been hiding the very thing God anointed you for?

Declaration:
I carry oil. I walk in authority. I refuse to blend in when I was called to break through.

"Touch not mine anointed, and do my prophets no harm."
—Psalm 105:15

Day 20: The Blood Still Works.

Scripture Focus:
"And they overcame him by the blood of the Lamb..."
—Revelation 12:11

Hook:
The enemy's best weapon still loses to *blood already spilled.*

Devotional Thought:
Your greatest flex isn't your strength; it's blood of Jesus Christ. Not your hustle. Not your "I'm doing better." The blood. Period! That blood that covered every sin, shattered every curse, canceled every demonic debt, and declared you righteous before you ever got yourself together. You're not clean because you're disciplined, you're clean because Jesus bled violently for you.

One man spent his life trying to earn grace, serving, striving, and performing. Still haunted by the past, he joined the usher board, the parking lot ministry, sung on the men's choir, was part of the men's ministry, and prison ministry. He spent all his time trying to earn God's power. Then there was a man who killed someone, served time in prison because he was selling drugs on the streets of Baltimore who struggled with processing his pass of wrongdoing. One day, this brother, decided realized that he could stand under the blood and live out the rest of his life as a son of God. He understood that grace is not something we earn from God. Grace is the power to perform the works of God. It's what God extends when we come to the end of our strength. When we realize we don't have strength to perform. God's grace, His power is made perfect in our weakness. When put down his guilt and stood under the blood, he experienced a different covering.

That blood of Jesus speaks louder than your past. Screams louder than shame. It reaches further than your past, it reaches far into your future. It defends when hell accuses. It covers you when life exposes your nakedness and vulnerability. It marks and washes you and makes worthy, when you don't feel worthy. So, when the enemy shows up swinging, remind him:

- Your sins have been washed away by the blood!
- You're already covered!
- Already clean!
- Already claimed!

The blood still speaks, still works, and hell still hates it.

Reflection:
Are you still trying to earn what Jesus already bled for?

Declaration:
I'm covered, I'm clean, and I'm claimed. The blood still works.

"In whom we have redemption through his blood, even the forgiveness of sins." —Colossians 1:14

Day 21: Burn the Backup Plan.

Scripture Focus:
"No man, having put his hand to the plough, and looking back, is fit for the kingdom of God. —Luke 9:62

Hook:
As long as you have a Plan B, you will never give God your full "Yes."

Devotional Thought:
Half-commitment is spiritual sabotage. You cannot slay giants with one hand on the plow and the other on your past. You cannot break cycles while keeping your options open. Kingdom men do not entertain escape hatches, they burn them.

One man kept a Plan B, just in case purpose got hard. So, he took more time focusing on Plan B than he did for Plan A. He was taught that he needed a contingency plan for every area of his life because Plan A might not work. So, he played it safe, called it wisdom, but never walked in fire. He did not understand that walking with God requires us to walk in the fire because God is a consuming fire. You cannot walk with God and not feel the heat of His presence. On the other hand, his cousin was experiencing the same fears, pressures and thoughts of failure but recognized that every plan that God has is Plan A. God already included you failing in his plan. He already made space for your future mistakes. God already provide a clause for your mess-up. All things would work together for the good of those who God calls according to His purpose. So, the cousin torched his exit strategy and said, "If God called me, I'm all in." they had the same calling, same fear but different courage.

Purpose requires a kind of crazy that scares comfort and chokes out complacency. Walking in your purpose ain't no side hustle. This assignment requires all of you. Body, soul, and spirit. You do not need more options, you need obedience. You need a yes that does not come with a backup plan. So, stop flirting with fallback. Kill the safety net. Delete the exit plan. Shut the door, you keep pretending you do not want to walk through. You did not survive hell to live hesitant. You were called to go all in. It is time to move from ready, set! To GO!

No retreat! No reverse! No rival!

Reflection:
What "just in case" plan is blocking your breakthrough?

Declaration:
I burn the backup plan. I'm all in. No fear, no fallback, just fire.

"Trust in the Lord with all thine heart; and lean not unto thine own understanding." —Proverbs 3:5

Day 22: Hell Fears a Healed Man.

Scripture Focus:
"He healeth the broken in heart, and bindeth up their wounds."
—Psalm 147:3

Hook:
The most dangerous man in the world is the one who let God heal him.

Devotional Thought:
You are not soft for healing, you are strategic. Hell makes a fortune off unhealed men. Men who are angry but do not know why. Brothers who protect trauma like it is a personality trait and strength. Bruh, the enemy wants you bitter, insecure, emotionally numb because a numb man will not lead, love, or war right.

One man bottled it all up, called it strength, but it was just silence dressed in shame. Man, he carried that bitterness and insecurity into every relationship. He did not realize because he was not healed, he attracted women and friends who were not healed. He was experiencing that old saying, hurt people – hurt people. One day he was talking to his friend an noticed he was in a healthy relationship with a woman and was about to get married. He questioned his friend; how did you find this woman and this nice relationship. His friend responded, after my last relationship failed, I realized I needed to heal so, I talked to a counselor and decided to surrender my bitterness, pain and insecurity. I laid it at the feet of Jesus and walked out with power hell could not touch. Same pain but different posture and different result.

You do not need to fake tough. You need to get whole because a healed man leads right, loves right, and fights right and that terrifies hell. You do not conquer what you ignore, you conquer what you surrender. That rage, shame and wound that your father caused, let God touch it and heal it! Let Him tear it out. Healing is not weakness, it's warfare. And a healed man is a walking threat to every bloodline curse still trying to breathe.

Reflection:
What wound are you still hiding that God wants to heal?

Declaration:
I am healed, whole, and holy. I lead from my scars, not my shame.

"With his stripes we are healed." —Isaiah 53:5

Day 23: Authority Is not Optional.

Scripture Focus:
"Behold, I give unto you power..." —Luke 10:19

Hook:
You don't ask for authority; you walk in it.

Devotional Thought:
God did not save you to be timid, He called you to take over. This is not survival, it is territory taking. This is dominion. We are commissioned to bring the Kingdom of Heaven into the earth! This is war! Authority is not arrogance, it is alignment. You have been handed Kingdom rights, but if you keep walking like a slave, hell will keep handing you chains. Stop praying scared. Stop living soft. Stop bowing like God has not already crowned you. You are a King!

One-man begged God for scraps, hoping for mercy, waiting on breakthrough, praying like a tenant. He was acting like He was a stepchild. This guy did not understand that he is seated in heavenly places in Christ. Christ is seated on the right hand of God our father. If we are in Christ, we have access to God's presence. One day, he heard this man praying, declaring and decreeing like he was a King. He was amazed! He watched as the man stood like a son, declared like a king, and moved like heaven had his back. This man was not hoping for mercy, he knew that God already promised that goodness and mercy is following all the days of his life. So, he acted like it! He began to take territory for the Kingdom of Heaven. They had the same access but different aggression.

You carry the same power that raised Jesus from the grave. So, act like it. Demons do not negotiate with cowards. They do not flinch for the passive or flee from men who know who they are. So, own the room. Command the storm. Rebuke the cycle. Go boldly to the throne of grace! Heaven backs boldness. Always has! Always will!

Reflection:
Where are you walking like a servant when God called you a son?

Declaration:
I don't shrink, I command. I have Kingdom authority and hell knows it.

"Thou shalt also decree a thing, and it shall be established unto thee."
—Job 22:28

Day 24: Stop Waiting. Start Warring.

Scripture Focus:
"From the days of John the Baptist until now the kingdom of heaven suffereth violence, and the violent take it by force."
—Matthew 11:12

Hook:
Your miracle's not on delay, it's under attack.

Devotional Thought:
God's not stalling. You're just in war mode. Everything you've been praying for is already yours, but it's being fought over in the spirit. You're not being denied, just delayed by resistance.

One man kept waiting for open doors, asking for signs, watching the wind—paralyzed by the illusion of "timing." He sat waiting for God to do what he prayed for. He did not operate from the position that he needed to work and war while he waited for God to move. The other guy received the same promises and the same delays. Yet he understood that waiting on God is a posture of serving Him like waiters serve us when we go out to eat at a restaurant. This guy rose up, went to war, and pulled it down. See, God was the same in both situations. The difference in the equation was the guys. The one with the most grit commanded the blessing and received quicker.

Stop waiting for perfect conditions. Take it by force. Prayer is how you talk to God. Warfare is how you talk to demons. God don't need to tell you again that you are a man, son, king and priest again! You need to walk in it! Hell isn't about to hand you what God promised. You've gotta snatch it. Suit up! Put on the whole armor of God! Speak up! Show up and take what's yours, like a son, not a slave. This ain't passive. This is war. And the violent still take it by force. You are a taker for the Kingdom!

Reflection:
What have you been waiting on that God already gave you authority to seize?

Declaration:
I don't wait, I war. What's mine will manifest by fire and faith.

"Resist the devil, and he will flee from you." —James 4:7

Day 25: Stop Fumbling Favor.

Scripture Focus:
"See then that ye walk circumspectly, not as fools, but as wise, redeeming the time..." —Ephesians 5:15–16

Hook:
Favor will find you—but *discipline* will keep you.

Devotional Thought:
You've been praying for open doors—but let me ask you straight: Can you carry the favor when it shows up? Because God won't give you what you refuse to steward. You're asking for promotion with a lazy spirit and an undisciplined lifestyle and wondering why the door's still shut.

One man begged for elevation but wasn't built to handle it so when favor came, he fumbled it. God will open doors for some of us for us to walk onto the field to play in the game. Sometimes he grants us favor to crawl under the fence onto the playing field without anyone noticing. Whichever way He decides to extend favor, we must be prepared to leverage the opportunity and not fumble. When offered the same opportunity, another brother was ready for it! You see, he trained in the shadows, stewarded over the small, and when the door swung wide, he didn't walk through, he took over. He did not beg for elevation; he worked on the field and was trained to step into the position before favor elevated him into the position. That's what happens when opportunity is met with preparation. Same promise. Different preparation.

Favor is Heaven's "yes." Discipline is your response. You don't need more opportunities; you need more order. More structure. More self-mastery. More obedience when nobody's watching. Don't fumble God's favor', train for it and be prepared to step into it! Move like the door is already open and trust God to handle the hinges. Because what you're praying for isn't delayed, it's waiting on your development to catch to the promise.

Reflection:
Where has lack of preparation been costing you breakthrough?

Declaration:
I protect what God provides. I walk in wisdom, not waste.

"He that is faithful in that which is least is faithful also in much..."
—*Luke 16:10*

Day 26: Real Men Repent.

Scripture Focus:
"Repent ye therefore, and be converted, that your sins may be blotted out..." —Acts 3:19

Hook:
Repentance isn't weakness. It's warrior protocol.

Devotional Thought:
Fake men hide. Real men repent. Confession isn't weakness, it's warfare. It's not about shame, it's about ownership. It's about relationship and communication with God and ensuring we are in right standing with Him. He wants us pure! When we confess, he is faithful and just to forgive us! Hell wants you to be silent. Wants you fake. Wants you bound up with guilt so thick you smile in public and die in private. But repentance flips the whole script.

One man wore a mask and led with charisma, but his heart was rotting because he had what he thought was secret sins. He did not realize the simplicity of confessing to God what we did wrong puts us back into right standing. Because of his so called secret unconfessed sin, he was out of position. The dirt from his sin left him outside of the covering of God. Look Bruh, God stands ready to forgive us and to put us back in righteous standing with Him. We might as well take Him up on it! Because the other guy over there messed up to but, he dropped the act, confessed it raw, and walked out clean and covered. Same secret. *Different spirit.*

Man, when you confess, you reclaim power. You shut down hell's access and testimony. You give God full clearance to wreck every stronghold, destroy every yoke and rebuild your soul from the inside out. Don't sugarcoat your sin or justify it, Kill it! Change your thinking, turn away from it and get clean and free. Get fire!

Reflection:
What sin are you managing that God is commanding you to *murder*?

Declaration:
I repent. I renounce. I rise. Sin has no grip on my future.

"If we confess our sins, he is faithful and just to forgive us..."
—*1 John 1:9*

Day 27: You're Not a Project, You're a Weapon!

Scripture Focus:
"Thou art my battle axe and weapons of war: for with thee will I break in pieces the nations..." —Jeremiah 51:20

Hook:
You're not being fixed. You're being *forged*.

Devotional Thought:
You're not some pitiful project God is trying to patch together. You're a weapon, being forged in fire. Every hit you've taken, every tear you have cried, and every sleepless night you have endured was not punishment. That is your preparation.

One man thought the pressure meant he was cursed and he cracked under it, questioned everything, and stayed stuck. He always had negative things to say about his life. He complained so much that he forgot to thank God for the blessings that He poured into his life. He literally spoke things into his life that God never intended for him. While sitting at lunch one day, he noticed his coworker who always had a frown on his face because of life's challenges was not frowning anymore. Turns out, his coworker suffered some of the same pains and loses but decided to lean into the heat, and let God shape him into a sword hell couldn't stop. By leaning into the fire, he was leaning into God. Both men experienced the same fire but one finished stronger than the other.

My man, understand this:

- You're not random.
- You're recruited.
- God has more than enough for you to make it!
- You're being weaponized.
- You are God's answer to a demonic system.

The hell you survived wasn't just trauma. God was adding it to your resume. God isn't just restoring you; He's sharpening you. He's putting edge on your anointing. He's carving strategy into your scars. So, wear them loud. Let every mark shout: "I'm ready."

Reflection:
Where have you been calling yourself broken when God calls you *battle-ready*?

Declaration:
I'm not fragile. I'm forged. I am God's weapon of mass destruction.

"No weapon that is formed against thee shall prosper..."
—Isaiah 54:17

Day 28: Build the Altar, Not the Brand.

Scripture Focus:
"Seek ye first the kingdom of God, and his righteousness; and all these things shall be added unto you." —Matthew 6:33

Hook:
Your name does not break chains. His does.

Devotional Thought:
Stop chasing clout. Build an altar. A meeting point between heaven and earth. You weren't called to be famous; you were called to be faithful. Because the influence is cute... But it can't cast out demons.

One man built a platform, and that joker got the likes, the followers, and the noise. People commented and shared every post he made. He had what appeared to be a large following of friends. But when hell knocked, he had no weight in the spirit. One of his friends did not stand in the social media spotlight. He just stood in the fire of the Holy Spirit. You see, he not only built an altar, but he also became an altar. He became a meeting point that people on the earth could experience heaven through and now when he speaks, heaven moves, and hell flees. These guys had the same gifting they built on different foundations.

God isn't impressed by your views. He's moved by your obedience. Going viral can't break yokes. But prayer can. Before you go public, go private. Before you build a platform, build a prayer life. Because what you birth in secret in the spirit will always outlive what you post online. It's time to get low, right, and real before God in prayer. You don't need more attention; you need to become an altar.

Reflection:
What have you been building that God never told you to start?

Declaration:
I choose presence over popularity. I build altars, not idols.

"Except the Lord build the house, they labour in vain that build it…"
—Psalm 127:1

Day 29: Die Empty.

Scripture Focus:
"I have fought a good fight, I have finished my course, I have kept the faith:" —2 Timothy 4:7

Hook:
The real tragedy isn't dying, it's dying with purpose still in you.

Devotional Thought:
When it's over, don't let people mourn what you could've done. Make sure you don't leave this earth with oil still in your jar, vision still in your mind, and fire in your belly you never released. Die empty. Vision fulfilled with anointing poured out. Your legacy unapologetically complete.

One man played it safe. He talked big, moved small, and left potential buried beneath excuses. He did not realize he does not have time to talk about. You only have time to be about it! When God reveals purpose and direction, it is time to mobilize. This other guy recently buried his mother and father. So, he realized that timing is critical! He lived like time was bleeding and every moment mattered. So, he emptied the clip! He shot everything that God showed him in dreams, visions, and prophetic releases. You don't know when the shot clock on your life is going to run out so, you better shoot your shot while you can. Each of us has been given a life. You should plan to leave a powerful legacy.

Bruh, you don't get forever. Time is short and every excuse you make robs your grave of the impact it was built to carry. You were born to empty out. So, preach like heaven's open, build like hell's watching, and break curses.

Father nations and shake systems. Leave nothing on the table.

Understand this! You don't get to be passive and powerful. Pick one! Heaven is watching and hell is hoping you'll quit. Don't go out full of fire. Go out empty of excuse. Go out like you were born to blaze. Let's GO!

Reflection:
What gifts, ideas, or impact are you still sitting on?

Declaration:
I will die empty. I will pour out every ounce of what God gave me.

"To every thing there is a season, and a time to every purpose under the heaven..." —*Ecclesiastes 3:1*

Day 30: Hell Regrets Your Survival.

Scripture Focus:
"What shall we then say to these things? If God be for us, who can be against us?" —Romans 8:31

Hook:
You weren't supposed to make it. But now that you did... hell's shaking.

Devotional Thought:
The enemy tried it. Depression! Abuse! Suicide! Addiction! He threw everything at you and still couldn't take you out. You don't just have a testimony; you've got receipts for every payment. Every sleepless night. Through every silent battle and tear nobody saw your cry. You arrived, stamped and sealed SURVIVED!

My father was abused. He went through hell and stayed stuck, he made survival his identity and silence his strategy. He was quiet and subdued! He looked strong but the testing took his fire! He always reminded himself about the hardness of his journey. It took his motivation and zeal for God and his purpose. On the other hand, his brother experienced the same demons and the same darkness. But he rose. Reclaimed his voice, spoke, and fought back. He made hell regret not finishing the job. Same trauma. Different outcome.

Now that you've survived, it's time to take over. Every demon that tried to bury you just witnessed its own funeral. You were the man hell hoped would stay silent, broken, and scared. But God flipped the script and now you are not just breathing. You're armed, dangerous, and backed by Heaven. You're alive for a reason, now make hell pay!

Reflection:
What are you about to do that will make the enemy wish he killed you when he had the chance?

Declaration:
I survived for takeover. I rise with fire. I am the man hell hoped I'd never become.

"Greater is he that is in you, than he that is in the world."
—1 John 4:4

You're Not Done. You're Dangerous Now!

You made it through 30 days, but this isn't the finish line.
- It's the front line.
- You've been activated.
- You've been confronted.
- You've been commissioned.
- Now it's time to move like it.

You didn't come this far just to go back to blending in. You didn't get delivered to stay distracted. You didn't break the cycle to live casually. You were forged for fire, designed for dominion, and built to tear down what took generations to build and rebuild it in righteousness.

So, here's your call to action:
- Don't just read this, live it!
- Don't just break curses, start building legacy!
- Don't keep this fire to yourself, spread it!

Take this message and light up your crew. Send this to your brothers. Start a men's group. Lead a devotional and launch a movement. Because bloodline breakers don't just get free, they make sure everyone after them stays free.

You're the blueprint and the standard now. You're the evidence that God still raises up warriors and if you ever forget who you are, come back to do it again. Because the man hell hoped you'd never become is standing tall now. Let's build, lead, and break everything that needs breaking. In Jesus name! Amen!

—Willie G. Miller Jr.

About the Author

Willie G. Miller Jr. isn't just a preacher—he's a problem for hell. A bold voice in this generation, Willie is an author, mentor, and apostolic leader called to activate identity, uproot generational strongholds, and raise up men who walk in power, purity, and purpose. He's not interested in cute church culture or soft sermons—he's building Kingdom assassins with fire in their bones and deliverance in their mouths.

Through his teaching, writing, and mentorship, Willie equips young men to confront inner chaos, break toxic patterns, and embrace their role as sons, kings, and priests. With a background in ministry, leadership development, and prophetic instruction, he fuses real-life grit with deep biblical revelation to spark true transformation.

Whether he's mentoring one-on-one, preaching with fire, or launching disruptive Kingdom-based resources, Willie's mission is clear: Wake up warriors. Break bloodlines. Build legacies that scare the devil. He currently leads a movement of emerging Kingdom men across digital platforms and in-person gatherings under the mantle of spiritual formation and generational restoration.

Will is the founder of WillieMillerMinistries.com a hub for books, mentorship programs, devotionals, prophetic training, and raw truth that pushes people out of cycles and into destiny.